Summer Trouble

Jonny Zucker

Illustrated by
Paul Savage

FULL FLIGHT

Titles in Full Flight

Badger Publishing Limited
26 Wedgwood Way, Pin Green Industrial Estate, Stevenage,
Hertfordshire SG1 4QF
Telephone: 01438 356907. Fax: 01438 747015.
www.badger-publishing.co.uk   enquiries@badger-publishing.co.uk

Summer Trouble   ISBN 1 85880 922 3

Series Editor: Jonny Zucker.
Publisher: David Jamieson.
Editor: Paul Martin.
Cover design: Jain Birchenough.
Cover illustration: Paul Savage.

Summer Trouble

Jonny Zucker

Illustrated by
Paul Savage

Contents

Badger Publishing

Chapter 1 - Bad News

Tom's mum forgot everything.

- She forgot his dad's birthday.
- She forgot to make his packed lunch.

She even forgot to tell him about the visit from his American cousin Ben.

He found out one Saturday morning when he turned on his computer.

Tom

From:	ben623@aol.com
To:	tom58@hotmail.com
Sent:	5 July
Subject:	My summer in England

Hi Tom

You won't remember me, but I'm your first cousin from America. I last saw you when we were both about two years old.

Anyway, isn't it great about my trip over to England for the summer! I'm really looking forward to it.

Best wishes
Ben.

Tom wanted to send an e-mail back that looked like this...

Ben

From: tom58@hotmail.com

To: ben623@aol.com

Sent: 5 July

Subject: No You're Not!

Ben

You can't come and stay. There's three weeks left of school, and then it's the summer holidays. I'm going to be hanging out with my best mate Jeyram, and I've got no time for you.

My mum's told me nothing about your trip, so it can't be true.

Tom

"Oh yes," his mum said, after he'd run downstairs. "I was going to tell you about Ben's trip, but I kept on forgetting."

"But when's he coming?" Tom asked her.

"Next Sunday," she told him.

That was only seven days away!

"There's no way he's coming with me to school," Tom told her.

"Oh, I forgot about that as well," she said. "I've asked your teacher and she says it's fine for him to go with you."

Tom went up to his room to text
Jeyram.

```
I need u 2 help me
```

Two minutes later his phone bleeped.

```
will b over 2 u in
1 hour
```

Tom and Jeyram sat in Tom's
bedroom. Tom told Jeyram about
Ben's trip. Jeyram said it might be OK,
but Tom was in a really bad mood.

He was still in a bad mood eight days later on Monday morning, when he heard the front doorbell ring. He ran to look out of the window. There on the front doorstep was a tall, skinny kid with three big bags looking up at him and smiling.

Chapter 2 - Bully Watch

"Well come on Tom, help Ben with his bags," his mum called.

Tom went downstairs to meet Ben. He helped him take his bags upstairs to the spare room.

"I've got to go out for a bit," said Tom's mum, "I've forgotten to get anything for supper tonight."

Tom and Ben sat in the kitchen. Tom tried to make an effort and asked Ben about school in America.

Then Ben asked Tom about school in England. After ten minutes they'd run out of things to say.

"Why don't you two clean my car?" Tom's dad said, coming in from the garden. "I'll pay you for it."

"Don't want to," Tom said.

Just then, the doorbell rang. It was Jeyram.

"Let's go to the park," said Jeyram.

They kicked a football around in the park. Ben said in America it was called soccer. He was rubbish at it.

Ben told them American football was much better.

Tom gave Ben some money and asked him to go and buy them some ice creams.

"What are we going to do with him?" asked Tom, when Ben had gone.

Ben followed them around all day.

In the afternoon they were by the swings in the park, when they saw Barry Homes, the class bully walking over to them.

"Alright boys," smiled Barry.

"Alright," said Tom and Jeyram.

"Who's this?" asked Barry, pointing to Ben.

"I'm Tom's cousin from America," said Ben holding out his arm to shake hands with Barry.

"I didn't ask you to talk to me, American boy," said Barry.

Barry leaned forward and pushed Ben over.

Barry walked off to the other side of the park, laughing.

Ben stood up and brushed the dirt off his jacket.

"You shouldn't have talked to him," Tom said.

"How was I to know?" asked Ben.

Jeyram

From: tom58@hotmail.com

To: jeyram950@yahoo.com

Sent: 13 July

Subject: The worst summer

Jeyram

Today was only the start.

This is going to be the worst summer ever! Ben is going to follow us all over the place.

We must do something.

Tom

Chapter 3 - "I'll get you"

The next day Ben went to school with Tom.

Tom and Jeyram had agreed to get away from Ben whenever they could.

That day, they sat at a different table.

On Tuesday, they hid behind the bike sheds in the playground so he wouldn't find them.

On Wednesday, they ran ahead on the way home, so he couldn't catch up with them.

Tom

From: jeyram950@yahoo.com

To: tom58@hotmail.com

Sent: 16 July

Subject: Ben

Tom

So far so good!

Ben seems OK by himself, and we are having a good time.

The summer may not be so bad after all.

Jeyram.

On Thursday morning, when Tom got up and saw the e-mail, he sent a text message to Jeyram.

```
U R RITE. WE'LL B
OK.
```

"Shall I walk with you to school today?" asked Ben coming into Tom's room.

"Not today," said Tom pulling his jacket off the bed, "I've got to get in early to do some things."

At the weekend it was harder. Tom's mum and dad kept on trying to get him to do things with Ben.

Tom's dad again said he'd pay them to clean his car, but Tom said no, they had better things to do.

Tom did feel that he was being mean, but he didn't want Ben hanging around with him and Jeyram.

"Is everything going alright with Ben?" Tom's mum asked on Sunday night after supper.

"You haven't spent much time with him. You and Jeyram always seem to leave him out."

"It's OK," Tom told her. "Don't worry about it."

A few days later after school, as Tom and Jeyram were walking round a corner, Barry Homes was coming the other way. Tom bumped into him.

"What do you think you're doing?" Barry shouted at Tom.

"I didn't see you," Tom said.

"Just you wait 'til our class party," Barry hissed at him. "I'm going to get you there, you'll see."

Chapter 4 - The Party Fight

It was the end of year class party.

Tom's phone bleeped.

```
U R OUT OF ORDER.
I'LL GET U.
```

Tom showed Jeyram the message. They both looked across the room at Barry. He was holding his phone and staring at them.

Tom thought of an e-mail he would love to send to Barry.

Barry

From:	tom58@hotmail.com
To:	barry1@nasty.net
Sent:	24 July
Subject:	Leave me alone!

Barry

You are a bully. You pick on people all the time and it's a real pain.

I wish you'd just get out of my life and leave me alone.

Tom.

Barry came across the class.

"You pushed my drink over," he said, looking at Tom and Jeyram.

"No we didn't," said Tom. "You were on the other side of the room."

"I said you pushed my drink over."

Barry looked really angry. He lifted his arm in the air and was about to punch Tom.

Suddenly Barry's arm was pulled back and he was thrown onto the ground. Someone was holding his arm behind his back.

It was Ben.

Ben stood over Barry.

Barry started to cry. "Ow, you're hurting me," he sobbed. "Let me go."

"Only when you say sorry to Tom and Jeyram."

Barry looked at them. "OK. OK, I'm sorry."

Barry stood up, wiping the tears from his eyes. Everyone at the party was laughing at him. He ran out of the room.

Tom and Jeyram looked at Ben in a new way.

"That was unreal," said Jeyram. "Yeah," said Tom, "You were great. No one has ever stood up to Barry."

"No problem," Ben told them.

"Where did you learn all of that stuff?" Tom asked him.

"I do kung-fu back home," Ben explained. "I only ever use it if there's a bully to deal with. And Barry is a bully, don't you think, cousin?"

Tom patted Ben on the back. "Yeah, Barry is a total bully, cousin."

Tom smiled at Ben for the first time.

Chapter 5 - A New Plan

The summer holidays were the best ever.

When you got to know Ben, he was pretty cool.

He showed Tom and Jeyram some of his best kung-fu moves.

He showed them some punches, kicks and blocks. They tried them out on each other.

He still didn't understand football, but after about a hundred games, he became OK at it.

One day Ben came down to breakfast carrying his three big bags.

"I'm flying home today," Ben told Tom.

"Sorry I wasn't very friendly when you got here," Tom said to Ben.

"That's OK," said Ben. "It's been a great summer and we're friends now."

Tom's mum was taking Ben to the airport but she'd forgotten where she'd put her keys.

"They're in your pocket," said Tom's dad.

Tom waved as the car drove off down the street.

Ben

From:	tom58@hotmail.com
To:	ben623@aol.com
Sent:	25 August
Subject:	My trip to America

Ben

As your trip over here was so good, I think me and Jeyram should come to America next summer.

What do you think?

Tom.

Tom

From: ben623@aol.com

To: tom58@hotmail.com

Sent: 26 August

Subject: Your trip to America

Tom

Sounds good, but there's two things you need to know.

1.   If I was bad at soccer, (sorry football), you and Jeyram will be ten times worse at American football!

2.   We also have bullies here, so you better work on those kung-fu moves!

Ben.

Tom looked for his money box under his bed. If he and Jeyram were going to America next summer they'd need money. And lots of it.

There was only seventy four pence in his money box.

He ran downstairs to find his dad.

"Dad, I want to clean your car today," he said.

His dad looked up from his newspaper.

"You do?"

"Yes," Tom told him. "I'll do yours first, then mum's, then Mr. Smith's next door."

"Well then, I better get you some hot water," his dad said.

But Tom didn't hear. He was already running to text Jeyram.

With all of those cars to wash, he'd need some help!